SENZO

Everything I couldn't Say
Love, romance and the 'in-between'

"What I wanted to say , found its way. . .

When I pieced together some

beautiful words in a poetic way . Now

whatever I say, feels like a song of

night and day..."

- Senzo

This book is dedicated to those glimmering eyes whom I met a countless of times but maybe the address was wrong because I never truly reached them, maybe they lied to me, just like my heart did...
More importantly, this book is dedicated to all those sweethearts who dared to love because in the words of Keanu Reeves -
'If you can't fight for your love then what kind of a lover are you'
Finally, this book is dedicated to my 'heartbeat', my 'Gilahri', my sweet and petite, Shahad

"Even with those eyes, the heart is
blind...
Even with those thoughts, the mind is
blank,
But when it sees you, it starts feeling
what it couldn't think of,
And when it believes you, it starts
thinking of what it couldn't feel
enough"

— Senzo

Contents

Preface

This book is a culmination of every word that couldn't be said, every thought that couldn't be expressed and every love that couldn't flourish.

I wrote it when my heart has had enough and my mind was done thinking. It is basically a commentary between the two sworn enemies of a person, *the heart and the mind.* What follows is a story of romance which the heart experiences but the mind questions because *"As the heart starts to hasten, the mind starts to reason..."*

Apart from that, my sole intention of writing this book was to tell that *one person*, how much She mattered to me, I wish she knew that the letter which I handed her, wasn't the only piece of poetry I'd written for 'Her'. *I wrote a book instead...*

But none of this would matter, if not for my partner, my sweet petite babe, whose love had me finish this book. Yes, initially, this book was being written for someone, someone whose eyes had cast a spell on me but alas, *spells don't last long if the wizard is Gone...*

Therefore, I was in no shape to finish the story I had started through this book but thanks to my Partner, my sweet-sweet

Shahad, I was able to finish this book. Thus, if *She* was my *'Love that ought to be'* then my sweet *Shahad* is the *'Love that is...'*

I hope you all have a wonderful time *hoping, thinking, believing, crying and loving* while also being a *hopeless romantic* at the same time, while reading this book.

Acknowledgments

This book maybe written by me but none of it would be here, if not for my family, my friends, my love and my colleagues, who had time and again, inspired me to keep writing what I always wrote, *Love, romance and the 'in-between'.*

I would like to thank my friend Tathagat Singh, for being such a helpful hand in getting the entire draft ready for publication.

I would like to thank all the first batch of my 'reviewers' who had read the very first draft of this book and had given me a wonderful feedback, I guess most of them fell in love with not just the words but with someone special in their lives.

A special thanks to the Publishing team who gave me this opportunity to present this beautiful symphony of heart to you all, my beloved Readers.

And most importantly, I would love to thank God, it's all because of his blessings that I was even able to pen down a word. I consider myself blessed to have his existence in my life. Thank you God.

Prologue

"What I wanted to say , found its way. . .
When I pieced together some
beautiful words in a poetic way . Now
whatever I say, feels like a song of
night and day..."
- Senzo

❤❤

The name of this book shall be –
'Everything I couldn't say'

You know, love is something special.
   Either it exists or it doesn't, there is
   no in-between here .
   This is what makes love, a special
   thing .
   This is what makes it a rarity.

The heart and mind , they want to
   work together but more often than not
   we know that they just don't !

"Heart seeks love but the mind
   questions it"

In the realm of poetry and romance ,
   heart's job is to feel , feel that its alive
   for someone or has a reason to be .
   But mind ?? well, the mind isn't a very
   good friend of romance, coz it is
   'scared' of it or maybe 'scarred' by
   previous misadventures .

So what is my intention specifically to
   write this book ? Well, I just want to
   write love . I wish to express those
   things that usually aren't , because
   'the mind thinks a lot'. Even after
   countless 'hopeful' eye-contacts that
   may awaken a dead heart , it's the
   mind that wishes the heart to remain
   asleep.

Coz it very well, for a fact, knows
   that once this guy wakes up, he is
   gonna create a ruckus.

'Love is like a tidal wave , it
   comes in an instant and drenches
   you wet in affection ...'

But you see , often our 'feelings' are
   like 'id' that makes us think
   irrationally and feel endlessly .
   There is no limit as to what and till
   what extent a person may end up
   feeling when he falls in love.
   But, just like the tidal waves that
   cannot remain high all the time , so
   does love .

'Even a slightest
   contradiction to its desires ,
   makes it break like a glass'.

"Once shattered ,
   a glass cannot be struck together the way it
   used to be. Likewise, once broken,
   a heart can never be the same"

It is exactly why love isn't just a
   struggle between expectations and
   service, but also a struggle between
   'Rationality and feelings'.

The former works on facts and logic , the latter does on emotions and desires .

Thus –
   "Mind and heart are like fire and water …they can never be one".

Love , as long as it is being fed off its desires and expectations, becomes the strongest force for a man. But what if it isn't ? What if there is no love in one's life ? Well , here comes the *'tragic in romantic'* of love .

   "When I started feeling for you, I started thinking less … when I started seeking your validation , I started losing myself".

   Thus , one gets lost forever , only to be found by someone else …

One

The Wizard and it's sorcery...

The Wizard and its sorcery—

> *"Curious about the universe , I often*
> *witnessed the skies ...*
> *Little did I know , mine would be*
> *found in those eyes ...*
> *When I witnessed them up close , I*
> *saw magic,*
> *It was hella amazing while also*
> *being tragic ...*
> *The exposure to its sorcery drove*
> *me crazy and a bit poetic . . .*
> *Unfortunately , those cryptic spells*
> *and sorceries have made it*

complicated , whether to confess it?
Or to keep it concealed?
That you are the wizard who've
cursed me indeed".
-Senzo

* * *

-When I saw those eyes , I got lost…
   What a wild intoxication it was that
   for a moment I thought it was all I
   ever wanted . The desire to keep
   looking into them and dream, was surreal .

It would be poetic to say that –

   'Even for a split second of
      your eyes, I used to feel time
      slowing by, for a countless of miles...'

But you see , as time passed by ,
   I realized that this new addiction of mine
   isn't just romantic but also a
   bit tragic, coz even if you never
   realized it but your eyes used to
   reveal a lot… They always does . . .

'Words may lie but the eyes
      cannot'.

I realized that your heart used to
    beat so slow that you knew , its
    sleeping but you also were aware
    that it better be like that . . .

        'I read your story through
            them eyes, found you amidst the paradise of
            your eyes...
            You were hiding there in solace
            but how far would you go with
            those lies?'

I just wanted to let you know that I
    never wanted to let it flow . . . that
    you are the wizard , whose spells
    shackled my heart so tight that now
    its wide awake, that now it's wide
    open ... ready to be hurt again ...
    I want you to stab it right here...
    Coz I know , we don't have any
    story anywhere.

    "It felt like it would never end .
        Turns out , it had no end ..."

Coz it was me who found you but you
   weren't aware of my discovery, of you…

All I want to say is , I wish my story to
   be with you but I may not ask of
   anything from you…
   All I wish to confess is, *I love you...*

* * *

Two

Talking through the Eyes...

Talking through Eyes—

> *"We were quiet...but our eyes did*
> *the talking,*
> *Words were less . . . but the poetry*
> *sprung by them would suffice,*
> *They all witnessed them move but*
> *none knew the path they took...*
> *Seeing yourself in those eyes , Oh!*
> *what a wonderful look ,*
> *I still couldn't believe that a reflection*
> *of me would've had me shook"*
> *-Senzo*

10

Whenever we used to meet , I always
   ran short of words . . . It felt as if I
   had a lot to say but when I witnessed
   you, all went into hay.

> *"You left me short of words,*
>   *Those eyes mesmerized me,*
>   *Short of words but full of emotions,*
>   *They perplexed me..."*

The most romantic sensation that
   one derives while falling in love is the
   romantic poetry that is sprung by
   them eyes . . .
   Its like you just witness their eyes
   and feel something that maybe a
   lie but it makes you so high, so
   intoxicated… that you cannot help but
   get addicted .
   This is why , witnessing them is the
   cause as well as the effect of love.
   Therefore, it is often said that –

> *"I often preclude myself from*
>   *looking in her eyes,*
>   *Coz I am afraid I'll get addicted to*
>   *those highs"*

Love isn't found in words but in

the eyes.
Coz words may be deceptive but the
eyes cannot.

> *"The real magic lies , not in the*
> *words but in the eyes. Don't you see*
> *it?*
> *Then how would you believe it?*
> *Just look me in the eyes and witness*
> *the skies...*
> *Don't you know, who resides in those*
> *highs?"*

Of course it's you! Unfortunately you
haven't looked there yet, coz if you did then you
won't remain the same... you may
go insane.
This is why I often say –

> *"Eyes are the way to the heart...*
> *Be careful coz you may get hurt"*

What a peculiar thing it is to talk with,
not the words but the eyes...

> *" When two hearts wish to talk*
> *They need not use words to*

convey the message...
Rather, its those eyes that do the
magic..."

What a wonderful sensation it is, to
    be in a room full of people, bustling
    with crowd, where even a single
    word uttered by you would go
    unheard… Yet when your eyes
    meet theirs, it all makes sense . . .

You see –

> *"Words weren't even necessary*
> *for us to converse,*
> *Your eyes used to say and mine*
> *used to hear ,*
> *Your heart used to smile and mine*
> *used to bear"*

This is why, I firmly believe that
    talking through eyes is like telepathy, coz –

> *"I wouldn't say a thing and you*
> *wouldn't hear anything , yet it all*
> *made sense...*
> *Her eyes were like an incense, her*
> *smile was its fragrance"*

The conversation between two hearts
   is so romantic that if one smiles, the
   other gets ecstatic .
   If one cries, the other starts
   shedding tears…

You see –

   *"There is no privacy between
      hearts"*

But as there is always destruction
   after the storm, so is there a 'but' in
   every story, no matter what form…

Yes, eyes do not lie. But that
   doesn't mean that the heart cannot
   be fooled by them, coz –

   *"Eyes may deceive the heart ,
      They may baffle you into believing
      things that don't even exist coz
      heart is indeed the culprit"*

When the interpretation of eyes go
   wrong by the heart, you end up
   being extremely lost and hurt.

"Those looks , those beautiful
  eyes,
  I thought maybe I am the one for
  whom they'll shed tears and cries...
  Turns out, they were just filled
  with lies"

This is why there is always a conflict
  between the heart and the mind .

"Heart wants to believe the eyes ,
  mind focuses on its lies..."

* * *

Three

Finding myself in You...

Finding myself in You—

> *"Talking to you felt like talking to*
>   *myself...*
>   *Were you my mirror or was I*
>   *daydreaming?*
>   *It all seemed perfect as you*
>   *appeared to be my exact,*
>   *Just like a chord struck right out of*
>   *the blue , in the middle of nowhere"*
>   *-Senzo*

The first step after having those

poetic conversations through the
eyes is that of *'finding yourself in
them'*. Yes, it is true that the
opposites attract but what further
reinforces this attraction is getting to
know that what seemed different,
turned out to be so indifferent…

"When I first laid my eyes upon you,
I thought I was doomed...
You seemed like an antonym...
But little did I know that what seemed
so different would turn out to be so
indifferent,
That you'd come out as my exact
synonym,
And I 'll sing your name like my
favorite hymn"

Yes, opposites do attract but it's
those similarities that brings the
hearts on track.
Love is like a duality, it's a game of
guess, where you never know
whether you are actually seeing
yourself in them or just trying hard to. . .
Whether you are seeing your exact
reflection or just an enhanced
projection…

Thus, love is like a duality of
reflection and projection –

> *"I wanted you to be like me . . .*
>   *So that I can love myself better in you..."*

When we were kids , we didn't bother
   about what the world thought and
   how they saw us... But the tables
   turned when we grew older and
   failures started hitting us harder...
   When our fears chased us without
   losing tracks...
   We then started believing in the
   exact same lies that the world
   thought of and accepted the
   projection of what they saw in us.
   Thus we became what we truly
   were not.

> *"Amidst all this chaos, I forgot*
>   *myself...*
>   *And when I saw you, I started*
>   *learning you myself,*
>   *All in the hope that maybe you'd be*
>   *the medicine that I always needed...*
>   *Maybe you'll make me remember*
>   *myself when I truly hated"*

That is why , when one falls in love ,
    it is not that he fell in love with the
    other… It's the fact that he started
    loving himself after remembering his
    own-self. Because what he
    lacked , he found it in someone
    else.

"A new toy to play with . . .
    A new person to make his...
    This is where the heart wants to have
    its time,
    This is where it wants you to be mine"

Coz all this time growing up , its
    expressions were curbed… as the
    world had its opinions hurled,
    alongside its lies on it…
    So the mind took over…

"I started thinking more and
    feeling less ,
    My heart became a hopeless
    mess,
    Now only the mind can cure
    its uselessness"

Talking to you and getting to know ,

wasn't much... Now I wanted you to
be mine , as I couldn't have you
enough.

> *"What I lacked , I was searching in*
> *you...*
> *Little did I know that you yourself*
> *were lost,*
> *Maybe I should've understood you*
> *better,*
> *Instead of giving you a letter...*
> *A letter stating that – Now you are*
> *me and I am you , lets be each*
> *other since I Love you..."*

This is where it all went downhill...
What I wanted was myself but
through you...
And what you wanted was yourself
but through me...
But, we both didn't know that we
hated the idea of ourselves.

> *"We both were so similar that we*
> *hated ourselves*
> *While wanting each other in all its*
> *glory and color,*
> *Of course, we were on our way to*

butcher what was already there...
Yes, I am talking about Love... which was now
nowhere..."

As much as it appeals to fall in
   love, one must truly realize that it
   can't happen unless you know
   yourself and more importantly until
   you love yourself.

Coz love is like a mirror, it reflects…
   But if you hate yourself then it no
   longer reflects. Rather it projects…
   That is why it is often said that –

   "You didn't love them , you just
      loved your idea of them...
      Thus, the heart wishes to find itself but
      the mind knows that it hates itself"

* * *

Four

An unfinished poetry...

You, an unfinished poetry—

*"I often preclude myself from looking
in those eyes
Coz I am afraid , you'll see...
You'll see every bit of me,
You'll see every bit of you...
Lying there like an unfinished piece
of poetry,
Which is in perfect symphony and a
romantic symmetry...
Where I am the writer but the story
has to be you,
Of course , you are the secret that*

you never knew"
-Senzo

When our eyes meet, hearts talk
When our hearts talk , souls befriend
each other.

Loving someone means , also hiding
your eyes
Coz the eyes never lie, they reveal
you for who you really are... No matter
which words come out of the mouth,
its those eyes that will always shout.

One doesn't wish to be torn apart in
pieces...
But falling for someone , makes you
vulnerable,
Your way of interacting changes,
your personality shifts... Those
eyes are afraid to meet theirs but this
heart doesn't know patience.
All it wants is the symmetrical poetry
between the eyes, where -

" Our eyes wander a lot many places
But we both know , whom they seek
in all those places...

*Yes , its you , It has always been
you ...
But you are my secret that you
never knew..."*

We often believe love to be a thing of
　　physical realm where 'touch' is the
　　element of it and intimacy , its pure
　　state…
　　But, when the heart falls, it
　　doesn't care,
　　All it does is *'stare'*…

Stare in those eyes secretly,
　　hoping to find itself there, the way
　　it homes theirs in itself…
　　This is why , one becomes secretive,
　　Coz no one should know why this
　　heart was acting all fugitive.
　　Therefore, until and unless eyes
　　meet and the hearts start talking, the
　　poetry sprung by them remains an
　　unfinished masterpiece…

It's a romantic symphony composed
　　of emotions
　　But expressed out very thoughtfully.
　　This is where it loses, as the mind
　　isn't very good with expressions.
　　It's the hearts job to feel…

But oh dear, *heart's such a criminal,*
   It is guilty of falling for someone
   without their consent…
   It is a fugitive who went out hiding in plain
   sight,
   It doesn't wish to be caught, it doesn't
   wish to be left vulnerable coz love is
   an expensive venture , you never
   know when it becomes a
   misadventure…

* * *

Five

Poetic painter

Poetic Painter—

> ***"I wished to write a story, but I kept***
> ***writing your name,***
> ***When I started painting on a canvas,***
> ***I kept painting your flame,***
> ***When I closed my eyes in frustration,***
> ***what I saw wasn't just a hallucination,***
> ***but it was something wild, something***
> ***new . . .***
> ***It baffles me to say this but even after***
> ***changing my artistry, the art was you"***
> ***-Senzo***

When I started writing, I wished to
become a poet all in an effort that I'll
write you the way no one ever did, I 'll
express you the way no one ever
could.

    "But when my pen used to run,
       thoughts didn't come out, only your
       name did..."

The ink in it was magical enough to
have spilled what my heart wanted
to have, yet I kept writing in an effort that
maybe someday, I'll have what was
always mine, I 'll have you...
But the ink was pure and so were my
feelings...
Therefore, I became not just a poet
but *'Your' poet.*
You became not just my art but a
masterpiece...
one which I was
always going to adore.

But you see, *this mind isn't a fan of*
heart's artistry... It thought maybe
whatever the heart feels is just a
hallucination, it's just a myth, not
something that can be a conclusive
proof of my art being an artistry, not

just a mockery of its ego.

Hence, it started painting
    And oh boy, was it so wrong …

> *"When the brushes of mind started*
> *   dancing, what came out wasn't just a*
> *picture but a portrait, a portrait of*
> *someone, who was deeply adored*
> *by the heart .*
> *It baffled him so much so, thus-*
> *"He couldn't fathom that even after*
> *having changed its artistry,*
> *The art was you.*
> *Even after having forgotten, the*
> *memories still reminded him of*
> *you"*

This is when it realized that not
    always it has to be done its way.
    Sometimes, he should let the heart
    play.
    Sometimes, he should just be a
    poetic dreamer and paint his
    dreams through words.
    Sometimes, *he should just be a*
    poetic painter.

Poetic painter

***

Six

The Eyes in the Skies...

The Eyes in the Skies—

> "When my eyes are wandering
>   through the skies,
>   I wonder, what if her eyes are also
>   doing the same?
>   Yes, our eyes may never meet but
>   what if our thoughts do?
>   What if she is also thinking about
>   me?
>   Coz even if miles apart from each
>   other,
>   Our eyes still seek one another"
>   -Senzo

Sitting idle in the balcony, looking
  towards those beautiful evening
  clouds, the *mind started wandering…*

  *"What if their heart is also stupid like
    mine?"*

What if they're crazy like me and this
  heart of mine?
  This is when the heart takes over and
  starts feeling.
  This is where the mind aids the heart,
  a rare cooperation but a welcome
  one…

  *"What the heart wishes to see,
    the mind portrays the same in
    those skies…
    What is always there but couldn't
    be seen, it becomes the work of
    those eyes"*

As now what is being seen in those
  skies are not the clouds, but You…
  My heart is singing out loud,
  Singing the hymn of 'cooperation',
  singing the hymn of love . . .

*"Be my friend and we shall be fine
    Romanticize this friendship and I'll be on cloud Nine"*

*Eyes start seeking what obviously
    couldn't be found in those skies,
    Mind starts hallucinating with
    these lies...*
It wonders what if the same kind of
thought process is being reciprocated
by them, miles apart.
Coz it very well knows that the eyes
won't catch each other from this far
but the thoughts may very well.
Unlike heart, the mind knows about
the *'Collective sub-conscious'*, it
knows how the Universe works.
Unlike heart, the mind knows its
theories and propositions well. But what
about the heart then?

Well, the *heart is just a stupid lover who
    'knows nothing' but 'senses a lot'.*

It may not think wise like the mind but it
can dream crazily wild enough that
whatever it had in itself , starts
becoming a reality.
You see, dreams do come true.
Even unknowingly, it feels the 'Law
of attraction' up close and thus, it

constantly beats for them in a hope
that maybe someday, distance won't
matter, and they will hear it beating.

"Maybe someday, they'll beat
together"

And when there is no more distance
left between the hearts, it's those
eyes that compose their love –

"Albeit through the skies, they do
not lie...
When they see each other, all they
do is shy...
When we miss each other, they do
nothing but cry...
But no matter what, they still seek
each other up that high".

* * *

Seven

A toxic obsession

A Toxic Obsession—

> *"You're the thought that keeps me*
> *going in daylight,*
> *Yet it's the same you that doesn't*
> *let me sleep at night...*
> *Low key wanna have you in my arms*
> *Yet I keep pushing you away,*
> *Am I falling for you or is it already*
> *too late?*
> *Are you really 'her' or losing you is*
> *my fate?*
> *Feels like I am obsessed, maybe a*
> *bit depressed,*

Whatever it is, I like it this way...
Sometimes close, sometimes away..."
-Senzo

Oh what a toxic sensation your
    intoxicating thoughts had on me,
    I felt like *I am addicted even when*
    there was no substance abuse, just a
    wishful thinking and a bit of
    endless You…

It is often said that –
    "In order to succeed at something,
    one needs to be obsessed about it"

But how to even succeed at
    something so trivial yet so
    complicated like love?
    Will obsession play its part, or will
    it be a downfall of it all?
    The latter seems truer than the
    former. Obsession isn't good, it
    may seem beautiful at first but it's
    never healthy.

Heart wants peace yet it's at an
    unrest when the mind keeps
    thinking about someone

constantly…
It's a toll on heart as it is not used to
any contradictions, be it in reality or
in its dreams…

Whereas the mind, being a critical thinker he is,
    always thinks not what can go
    right but *'What can go wrong'*…
    And this is where it all goes in vain as
    the 'two' starts clashing over dreams
    vs expectations.

Heart only 'dreams', Be it a dream
    with open eyes, when it witnesses
    theirs and starts beating faster… or a
    dream of night, where all the
    boundaries fade away and all that is
    left are those wild and sensational
    feelings… where the story is written by
    him and the pleasure is derived by
    the senses , notwithstanding the fact
    that it's not real,

> *"Heart doesn't work on facts rather it
>   stems off 'feelings'. What it feels,
>   has to be right, it knows no
>   contradiction…"*

Enter mind… when the senses have
    had enough of those fairy tales

sprung by the heart…
it starts thinking 'rationally'.
This is where it all goes
haywire, as -

> *"The world created entirely of*
> *feelings can't be defined under the*
> *paradigm of rationality"*

It doesn't work that way, This is why,
the *heart starts crying when the*
mind starts thinking .

> *"All I dream t of you, faded away*
> *when I started obsessing over*
> *you…"*

This is why, as long as the heart is
dreaming, stomach gets those
butterflies, but the moment mind
intervenes, eyes get those tears…
Coz the heart is like a child wanting an
ice-cream with a cherry on top of it…
Whereas, the mind is that adult who
knows that ice-cream won't last long
the way it is, it 'll soon start melting at
some point and thus the cherry would
fall…

This is where it contemplates the
    extremely 'Slow-motion' styled
    situation of heart in a swift manner,
    coz it is afraid that time doesn't wait
    for anyone, so it better be swift.

> *"Heart wants whatever it can have*
>   *now,*
>   *Mind contemplates the ending"*

> *"This is why, what seemed beautiful*
>   *when the eyes started meeting, became*
>   *a nightmare when the mind started*
>   *obsessing"*

> *"You seemed like her but maybe I*
>   *wasn't him.*
>   *I wanted you to be mine but maybe*
>   *I wasn't the one"*

This is why, when one falls for
    someone, distance becomes
    inevitable, it is that friend whom you
    may not like but the one whom you
    will need.
    Since, no one wants to be exposed of
    their desperation.

But you see,

> *"Heart hastens but the mind*

reasons,
Even then the heart just wanted a
dream, but the mind gave it a
nightmare"

"This is why, I was never really there.
When you used to pass by, my heart
used to skip beats…
No wonder, even if jokingly, you
called me 'heartless' coz when you
used to be around, it used to stop
beating.
Not coz it didn't have
anything for you, but the mind made
it believe that way…

Mind said,
"What will you do when
the things you wish won't be
reciprocated by her heart?
The heart knew it was a lie but even
lies have to accepted at times coz the
reality is far from beautiful
sometimes"

> *"When I was getting butterflies*
> *dreaming of her...*
> *She used to get moths"*
>
> *- The mind*

But even in this truth, the heart could've
found its solace coz its realm
knows no boundaries and only knows
how to 'give'.
It's the galaxy of mind, that creates a
ruckus. It invades the realm of heart
by its toxic and obsessive thoughts ,
and questions the very basis of its
existence ,

> *"The heart just beats but the mind*
> *questions it...*
> *Since it believes it all to be*
> *temporary... It asks the toxic*
> *question of "until when..."*

* * *

Eight

Hide and Seek...

Hide and Seek between your eyes and mine—

"We keep seeing each other in
dreams yet why is that not a reality?
You avoid me, I avoid you,
Is there really any clue?
Why is there such a duality?
Our eyes never meet
But we both know whom they seek...
Since no contact, is there really
anything intact?
Maybe you just mask it all,
overwhelming emotions cask it all...
Coz when eyes meet, hearts talk

> **But when hearts meet, souls talk.**
> **Therefore, I'll be on stalk,**
> **Who knows, maybe one day we can**
> **talk?"**
> **-Senzo**

When our eyes started meeting, my
  heart started singing…
  It was such a melodious hymn that I
  couldn't help but sing…
  Your name became a chorus of that
  song which would be like a prayer to
  me…

Your arrival in my dreams was like a
  daily ritual that it became a cult
  obsession for me.
  I left all interest in the day coz it was
  the night that had my heart pray…
  Pray that it's you again, tonight in my
  dreams coz the day was just a wind
  of 'dry air' but the night?
  Well, night became the wind of
  monsoon for me…

Ironically enough, when eyes used to
  open, a weird but obvious realization
  used to occur that –

"The dream is over, now I just have
to wait another endless day to
pass by, so that finally the night
comes by... where I'll be with
myself again, trapped with you...
where you wouldn't shy away from
letting those eyes meet mine and
letting your heart sing a duet with me,
like you don't in reality"

Reality became a disappointing
mess, but the night was just like a
wild guess...
I never knew, how our eyes were
going to collide and how we would
improvise in such an accident.
Although not a fan of bad omens but
this accident was an exception.

"I wanted to be injured by those eyes..."

Unfortunately, you somehow knew
about this new fetish of mine, this
new addiction of mine and in reality,
when you used to come in front of
me, eyes used to panic!

"Oh what a tragedy that my eyes
were getting a heart attack..."

Although its not surprising coz the eyes
are nothing but the extension of heart
in the realm of romance…
Coz eyes lead to heart…

Fine, I plead guilty. But what about
you? What illness were you suffering
from, when my eyes were getting a
heart attack?

*"Maybe you were also a patient like
me, but not a patient of me...
unlike me, who was a patient of
you...and not a patient of someone
else.
Maybe you were injured by
someone else' eyes...
Or maybe someone else first 'heart'
you and then 'hurt' you coz their mind
wasn't accompanying their heart,
when the latter was falling hard for
you...
It's alright, I understand this game
very well.
I love playing it even when I am
always the one losing... I am losing
this game to you, with you.
Coz maybe you wanted to win it but unfortunately, with
someone else..."*

But like they always say –

"The only way to win is by not
quitting..."
And this is why, I am always on
watch, who knows that maybe you'll
catch me looking at you?
Or maybe you already know that I am
on stalk ?
So, let's just wait till the day when
we 'll finally talk.
Lets just be patient until this Hide and
Seek between you and me is over,
and this time instead of losing it ,
I'll end up winning... winning your heart,
at least that is what I wish" .

* * *

Nine

The search...

❧❦❧

The Search for a 'perfect' You—

> *"What I lacked in myself, I kept*
> *searching in you...*
> *Little did I know, you yourself were*
> *lost, only to be found by me...*
> *But no matter how poetic it all may*
> *seem, it's still tragic in its conception*
> *and theme,*
> *That you didn't believe in me as*
> *much as I did in you... Maybe it was*
> *my fault that instead of fixing you, I*
> *fell for you...*
> *But you see, it is all coz of my belief*

that imperfections are beautiful...
And as an artist who adored beauty, I
thought maybe I could adore you the
way no one could,
Coz even in your darker shades of
hopelessness, I saw hope...
Coz in you, I saw us"
-Senzo

I was like a puzzle, whose integral
parts was lost.
Yet this case was a different fiasco
altogether as even I didn't know what all
was lost and what to even search
for?

"But the moment I saw you, I legit felt
like you were the missing piece of me
who was going to make me whole.
Maybe you were the rhyming that
was going to complete my song, a
clue that was going to solve this
mystery..."

But all this was the mind's work.
Heart accepted the way you were

and fell the moment it realized that
maybe it could heal someone like
you. But you see, the mind started
wandering as to how can I make use
of this situation and get you close to
me?

*Instead of fixing you, which was the
plan of heart, to be executed by
the mind... I fell for you which was a
blunder caused by heart's affection
towards yours.*

Mind had a plan that first, it'll fix
what's wrong in you and then mold
you the way it imagined you.
But you see, *this is why heart is
special*, instead of doing what the
mind wanted it to, it just fell hard and
realized –

*"It's better to accept someone the
way they are than to mold
someone into someone, whom
they clearly aren't"*

Heart saw those imperfections as
things of beauty but the mind on the
other hand saw those imperfections

as *"pebbles in its way of seeing
you clearly..."*
It thought that in order to see you
perfectly, there can't be any
imperfections.
In order to have some
reasoning as to why it should like
you, there has to be some tweaks in
you…

> *"Maybe to it, you were a flawed
> masterpiece...
> But to the heart, you were just an
> art who needed some adoration"
> Maybe we all do... Sometimes, fixing is
> not something that one needs but it's the adoration
> for who they really are, is all they desire"*

> *Since-*
> *"Imperfections are beautiful"
> But you see, the mind doesn't
> understand the heart coz the former
> 'thinks' while the latter 'feels'...*

But maybe you never listened to your
heart. Maybe all you did was follow
the errands of your mind, which
clearly didn't understand that –

*"In order to truly love someone,
 one shouldn't judge for **what is not
 there** but accept **what is...**"*

After writing all this, I finally
 realized that you were the one who
 was missing from me.
 Coz when I accepted you,
 I accepted myself...
 *When I understood you, I
 understood myself.*

* * *

Ten

Tables turn when it's love's turn...

Tables do turn when it's Love's due turn—

> *"The way you started admiring my*
> *words,*
> *Made me realize that words can*
> *mend broken things*
> *It's as if you were reading between*
> *the lines and I was the 'writing'...*
> *As if I was a poem and you, its*
> *writer...*
> *How the tables turn that the writer*
> *becomes a reader and the reader*
> *becomes a writer ...*
> *Tables do turn when it's love's due turn ..."*

-Senzo

The state in which I used to write,
   I wanted to feel complete by writing
   those words which I couldn't say …
   The previous time I fell for someone,
   I couldn't stand up… *Its not as if my*
   feet were injured but it was the heart
   that just wanted to beat for someone, **maybe**
   someone else...

   "Oh what a tragedy, for whom I
      wanted to beat, beat me so harsh
      that now I am scared to beat again"

   - Heart

Words were my only hope until I met
   you…
   Now, you became my sunshine
   In mornings, *you used to rise from*
   the east and then hover all around
   me elliptically until evening ... where
   you set yourself into a transition. As I
   wrote –

*"She nourished me like the sun
and now she is going to drench
me wet in affection with her tidal
waves of affection... She literally
became my moon by the night"*

Her love was intoxicating… it was like
a drug where, when she came
around , I felt like I was getting high…
And when she used to go, I felt so
low…
Its like her moonlight was my drug,
her adoration towards me was my
new addiction.

Oh, what a tragedy, I thought only
words through my ink would heal
me …

*"Turns out , **someone else**
thought otherwise , turns out …
someone else wanted to write
something else"*

It was **something new** which I never
knew … that it could even happen,
where I'd want to write a lot, but
words won't come out …
Not coz I was speechless, but I was

mesmerized and dazzled by her…
Maybe she was the writer now and I
was the reader…

> ***"Maybe she was going to write me***
> ***the way I wanted to write someone***
> ***else,***
> ***Maybe she wanted to love me the***
> ***way I wanted to love someone else…"***

Her presence was infectious, as now
   I wasn't that **same writer I used to be.**
   Now I became a poet…
   The Poetry which I wished to write,
   was standing right in front of me…
   I was baffled and speechless
   What could I even write when my
   imagination was now a reality…
   What could I even say when my
   words were stolen by ***someone else?***
   All I could do was, see the table's
   turn…
   Maybe it was my turn … my turn to
   read,
   My turn to feel my own words but
   by someone else' narration.

   "I write words but maybe you write me,

Tables turn when it's love's turn...

*I complete sentences but maybe
you complete me".*

* * *

Eleven

The Moon and the Moonlight

She became my moon and Her eyes were the moonlight—

"Even amidst the darkness in
those surroundings,
I witnessed those eyes...
Peeking into them made me feel a
kind of desperation,
A desperation so deep that I knew,
those eyes wanted to see more of
them...
More of them in more of mine.
That is how my eyes became a
mirror
That is how I began painting you a

> *river,*
> *A river of words, where the flow*
> *was towards you,*
> *Since I was the writer, but the*
> *book was you"*
> *-Senzo*

Love always flourishes in random,
  unexpected scenarios… It usually is
  found where and **when you least
  expect it.**
  Such was the moment when I
  realized **it's you**.
  When we met, the lights were a bit
  dim, the surroundings were a bit
  tense but what was so calm and
  intense, were your eyes…
  I witnessed them up close without
  even realizing that I am peeking into
  the most beautiful sea …
  I could see the tides rising in that
  sea,
  They moved like water to the oceans
  High and low, thanks to the moon
  I smiled in adoration and told myself–

> *"The peace I was searching for,*
>   *would be found in the most*

complacent way...
Oh, the irony that what I concluded
to be peaceful would turn my heart
into a havoc.
But this storm wasn't a bad omen
*Rather, it was **a new beginning**"*

Now, the mind and heart wanted to team-up **again**...
Since both of them adored the view
which those eyes portrayed them.
Mind agreed not to think much,
Heart agreed not to feel much...
But both the losers knew, it wasn't
going to last long , sooner or later
they're going to blame one another
for this pitfall...

"A lunge into the depths of her
eyes"

All the mind would remember, what
it thought when it witnessed those
eyes; all the heart would do was
miss how it felt to be a guest in
those eyes …
Now, the mind **concluded** that she
was the moon as she seemed
mysterious even in those dark times
where no mystery was left unraveled.
The heart **realized** that not her, but

those eyes would make it rush like a
moth to a night lamp…
Maybe she wasn't just a 'Night lamp'
in my darkness but much more…
maybe she was the moonlight of
my world…
Maybe she was **my new world...**

After all, the insect of love finally bit me again.

***

Twelve

Arrival of a heart...

Arrival of a heart which seemed like it wouldn't 'hurt'—

> *"She came in like a 'present' and made*
> *me admire my present.*
> *I used to write everything tragic, from*
> *heart to a heartbreak,*
> *From romantic to tragic ...*
> *From Mediterranean to Adriatic,*
> *Now all I wish to write was, 'Her'.*
> *All I wish to write was a love story,*
> *Where I would be the writer, but she*
> *would be the reader,*
> *Where I would be the book, but she*
> *would be its cover"*

-Senzo

'Magic which used to be tragic,
   Now became romantic ...'
   The moment you came around,
   things started making sense ...
   My words became meaningful
   when you started reading them...
   What a peculiar way of admiring
   someone when you read what I
   write with that much passion ...

I wish to write for you, but I am
   afraid... afraid that you will one day forget
   reading ...
   One day you will get pale with my
   words...
   Nonetheless I wish to keep
   writing as that is my only
   solace ... *coz the other one is*
   you.
   Either I can write you or have
   you...
   Coz the last time when
   someone loved reading my
   words, I mistook it for their
   passion of reading me ...

So, I wish to be cautious since I

cannot afford another isolation
from **my newfound solace.**

Here, the heart was like a child
again.
As if a lost child found its mother…
But oh what an irony, this time
the kid lost it's last mother, it's last
caretaker –

*"Now all it cared that **finally** it
would be taken care of…"*

On the other hand, the mind was
in a panic…
It knew that what
seemed entirely new is nothing
but the way of history.
History tends to repeat
but so does the heart…
Heart tends to repeat it's mistakes too…
Coz it doesn't understand
time…
For it, everything in front
of it is real, who takes care of it,
is authentic and who hurts it ,
is bad …

But the mind doesn't work on that

principle. It very well understands
time…
**"It knows that what is today will be
history tomorrow"**
Nonetheless, the battle continues …

Both hate each other, but both go
silent when a **new found home** is
what they sense…

> *"The mind thinks of its new found
> place, the heart feels of the
> warmth that it shall be getting
> once in there …"*

That is why the relationship between
heart and the mind is similar to that of
Tom & Jerry.

Both hate each other, but both can't
live without each other too…

> *"Coz what the mind couldn't think of,
> Heart senses… and what the
> heart couldn't feel enough, mind
> overthinks…"*

This is why love is like a poison, *you*

know it's going to leave you
vulnerable, but you love the feel of it.

You like feeling butterflies coz of that
heart and imagining romantic scenarios
coz of that mind.

Nonetheless, every broken heart and a lone mind deserves a good home...
A new Home.

***

Thirteen

The Prison and it's Poison...

Heart is a prison and your eyes are it's poison—

"You wish to drown in my eyes,
I wish to drown in yours...
The way you look at me, makes me
feel like water...
Would you like to drink from me?
Oh, I'd love to share
So why not just drown into each other
and care for one another?
You on top of me, I inside of you...
Drink me like a potion and come
again when you feel hurt
Since I am the well, which will never

> **go empty, so long as you wish only to**
> **drink from me"**
> **-Senzo**

<u>All of a sudden, it was a new Autumn.</u>
When she used to look at me, all my
senses became senseless .

   "As all I saw was her, but what my
    heart fell was her heart"

I couldn't help but feel the presence
  of something that wasn't there but
  then I realized that it's just my mind
  imagining us…
  Imagining her in a way
  that only I wished to see…

   "Her, on top of me …
    slowly drowning in my sea"

Our chemistry would be like fire and
  water.
  She be the fire and I be the water…
  Fire can be set above water, but it
  cannot touch it,
  Coz the moment it

does so, it loses its heat…
It becomes pale… **as the water
now takes the wheel…**

Love is that poison which one
   wouldn't want to drink but the way it
   makes them feel, they get addicted to the same.
   Maybe her fires were getting addicted
   to my waters coz she liked how the
   latter would calm the former.

*"Her flames would be in vain
   inside my waters … maybe she
   liked it being calm and pale for a
   while, maybe she was tired being
   this Lava and now wanted to feel some
   frigidness. Maybe she wanted to
   be bitten by my cold "
Oh, the irony, I ended up describing
her the way I wanted her to be with
me"*

*"My mind ran places and found
   one in her heart.
   My heart felt a lot of braces but got
   chained inside her head"*

*"How peculiarly strange, that my
 mind was in love with her heart and
 **my heart was now a slave to her
 mind"***

That is why we say,

**"Opposites attract.
 But we often forget that once tangled,
 they do not retract".**

I was heels over head **all again,** Maybe **'my end'** found its 'new
beginning'.
 Maybe my end became a new beginning…

* * *

Let's smile on each other...

Lets smile on each other so that my lips smear on yours—

Witnessing your face made me
realize, it will look good alongside
me...
Witnessing that smile made me
wonder, it will look good on me...
So, lets smile on each other, where
my lips would be yours and yours
would be mine,
Let's taste each other like a fine
wine"
-Senzo

<u>This Autumn was the new Summer ; Finally my 'Fifth Season' found me</u>

What a wonderful sensation,
 seeing your face… I felt like a
 spectator, witnessing true art in a
 museum full of cheap filters.
 What I saw in you, was nothing short
 of gorgeous. Its not that there aren't
 other beautiful faces to adore but
 yours was special coz your eyes
 showed me something that those
 faces did not.
 Something that my last time did not.

Your eyes showed me myself in such
 a beautiful way that I wanted to keep
 staring at my reflection as long as we
 didn't blink…
 As our interactions became frequent,
 something started to change … Now
 its not just my reflection which used
 to be seen in those eyes but *'us'.*
 Now I didn't just see but dreamed,
 looking at you… *looking at us.*
 Everything you… everything 'us'

From your eyes to lips, everything
 seemed perfect.

 Watching you smile, made me a bit restless…

You were miraculous and breathtaking,
Curvy and ferocious, bold and brave...
I believe you were my Nile.
I wish I could contain you in a vial...
Like a sunflower to the sun,
I was drawn towards You...
And all of a sudden, I was young...
Maybe, my dial stopped working,
Or maybe, it was all again...
Either way, my Heart was confused,
Whether to keep beating or to stop and admire,
Again and again...

When my heart used to feel that
smile, my mind wanted to imagine
something…

"What if we smile together?
What if we smile in such a way
that our lips move together in a beautiful
yet chaotic way? No but, no may..."

- The Mind

What if I grab you by the waist and slurp you like wine?
Smear my lips all over your you and have you dine?
Would it suffice? or you're already mine?

> *"Since we both knew that it'd be*
>   *sinful but now that everything seems*
>   *miraculous, why not try sinning*
>   *together and make it look like a*
>   *virtue?"*

Coz-

"Darling, everything is fine and fair in love and war,
    Everything vice is a virtue with you my love"

> *"So you be my wine and*
>   *I'll be the wine sommelier,*
>   *I'll keep tasting it and let you know,*
>   *How fine of a wine you are my Love...*
>   *You be that apple and I'll be your Eden,*
>   *Let's make us, each other's heaven"*

Love is that sensation, which at first
    seems so high that you wouldn't want
    to be apart...
    Usually it's coz the heart
    has clanged on to theirs and the mind
    overthinks that *'What if our bond*
    would be lost if we are kept apart?'

*"But you see Love, love is like a fine wine... it gets better
with time...
That is why two hearts would only
wish to taste their respective
minds, coz that is what they love to dine"*

The **mind knows how to imagine**
and imagination has no bounds… no
limits.
Thus, imagination is sexy and
hence the **mind is sexier** .
But the **heart knows how to feel**, and
it can feel almost anything the mind
comes up with, hence **the heart is
sensual…**

Therefore, in order to be sensual,
one needs sexuality, and in order to
be sexual, one needs sensuality.
That is why I say, both are a duality.

*"When I saw your heart, my mind
wanted to touch it … when I
saw your mind, my heart wanted to
make it mine,
Be my virtue and I'll be your vice,
Dance with me and I'll make you mine…"*

I further write…

> **"From toe to chin, let's be one and thin…**
> **In lights all dim, let's commit a Sin…**
> **Who knows, what lies beyond those eyes?**
> **Be my Virtue and make me your Vice"**
>
> **—Senzo**

Finally, I became one with *Her. Our virtues became one but the vices remain none.*

That is why Love with the right person is essential.

> **"She is everything that I am not.**
> **What was ought, never came to fruition,**
> **But what came to be, became a beautiful Sensation"**

Now I was no longer a writer, I became *Her Writer.*

* * *

Fifteen

Epilogue

A writer's power lies in the *process*, the *means* of getting love, falling for it and finally having it but not in the *ends* of it. Thus, what had been written here is basically what happens *before getting your love* because '*their thought is like a poison, the more you have it, the more you want*'. This thirst is only quenched, once you have your 'love'. Once you get intimate enough to let them know —

"*what your heart had felt, your mind had thought and your body had craved...*"

I write,
   "It's not you, who've had me awake but it's those memories that don't let me sleep"

Because once that is done, there is no incentive to write. ***All***

the beauty lies in the journey, not the destination.

Therefore, this book begins with a beautifully drafted scenario of a wizard and its sorcery but by the end of all this, its not the magic of that wizard that can be felt but the beauty of the reality *That IS...* When a person finally meets their match, whom they never searched but merely *found,* they get to break the vicious cycle of a Toxic love i.e., *seeing them-wanting them-chasing them-losing them-losing yourself entirely in the process.* This vicious cycle of love starts when you start losing yourself in the hope of 'finding them', *Your Love that is ought to be.* But the *Love that IS,* is the most beautiful and ultimate form of love because you didn't search for them, you just found it. It just happened. It just flourished…

Now, *Your Love that IS,* will help you create your very own, beautiful cycle of love i.e., *Seeing them-meeting them-knowing them-and then finally realizing that all you had been reading this whole time wasn't for the 'Love that ought to be' but for the 'Love that IS',* meaning thereby, What one believes to be love, might not be. This is why in the beginning itself, I warned every hopeless romantic who would be reading this book that *'If love is romantic then there is also a part where it becomes tragic'.* It is exactly why I often refer to the 'meeting of eyes' as an accident because it might seem beautiful but is clearly not. This is the *tragic in romantic* of falling for the eyes.

Yes, this whole time, I had been advocating for the

> beauty that is 'seeing yourself in those eyes' but you all must understand, *What we often see is just a reflection of us in their eyes... Eyes are a beautiful phenomenon to fall in love with but they clearly aren't accurate.* If people can't see properly even after putting on glasses then what are the odds that they will *'see the beauty that is You',* yes you are beautiful but never fall for the eyes, because eyes can be deceiving... It is often said that 'Through eyes, only the desires take form' and they always lead to disappointment because you thought maybe it was Love but turns out, it was just a wishful thinking, an imagination with no body...or may even be *Lust.*

Real love doesn't happen because it *should,* It happens because *it had to.* That's it. No one could ever explain *Why love happens* because it looks scientific but even science couldn't ever explain it. The only plausible clue that I found about it's 'reasoning' is derived from a film that too a *science fiction* one,that is-

"*Love transcends dimensions*"
  -*Interstellar (2014)*

And how can we even forget that beautiful line from Ed Sheeran
—

"People fall in love in mysterious ways..."
  — *Thinking out loud,* Ed Sheeran

I would like to thank you and congratulate each one of you, who are reading this, *yes you are special and Yes you are beautiful.* No matter how many times you would've had that 'accident of eyes' but always remember, you all survived … and one day, you wont happen to be in an accident of eyes because that time, It would be your heart that'd be colliding with another heart, beating together as if they are one. To conclude, I'd say—

"Sometimes broken words can mend broken hearts...
Sometimes even a flawed character can make someone's existence whole.
All you need is that missing piece to complete the puzzle which you have been...
All you need is someone willing to be keen...
Since, we all are like ocean, full of mysteries but not everyone can venture that deep,
Not everyone can be a mind to your heart and a heart to your mind"

— Senzo

But before marking the end of this book, I'd like to mention two poems for two special persons, **My Love that could've been** and **My Love that is.** The former taught me how to weep in silence, the latter taught me how to smile in open. One made me write this book, the other let me finish it. One made me an addict, the other came in like a rehab, One was cigarette, the other was nicotine. One behaved like the Sun, the other became my Moon.

Dear ***Love that could've been***,

> *"I tried being secretive about You but I failed at it terribly,*
>   *Coz the world caught me smiling at your reflection in my heart's mirror...*
>   *Now that there are no more secrets and the mirror being shattered to pieces,*
>   *I became creative and started writing those stories which could've been our secret,*
>   *Stories that could've been our Love Song..."*
>
> *— Senzo*

Dear ***Love that IS***,

> *"My poetry became a poetess and started writing me the way I wished to write her,*
>   *Now a writer became a reader and a reader became a writer...*
>   *What an artistic side of her that I became my own admirer..."*
>
> *— Her Senzo*

This is how, one made me a *Writer* and the other made me a *Reader*.

* * *

Sixteen

...

The reader with the writer

* * *

About the Author

Hey everyone, I am Aditya Pal. I like to call myself *Senzo*. I am a Lawyer by profession and a Writer by passion. The reason why I write is, to express what usually isn't said and more importantly, to make people fall in love with the 'process' of falling in love. Love is a complicated mess and so is the heart. The language of it is quite romantic while also being tragic. It is an aftermath of an 'accident' that takes place when two pair of eyes meet. *This 'meet' is where it all begins, this meet is where it all ends.* My poetry falls somewhere in between. I hope you enjoy *falling in love again*, I hope you are able to *live again*.

You can connect with me on:

https://www.facebook.com/aditya.pal.376

https://www.instagram.com/i_am_maverick_sen

www.ingramcontent.com/pod-product-compliance
Lightning Source LLC
Chambersburg PA
CBHW031452150726
47990CB00007B/2724